The Shoemaker and the Christmas Elves

Illustrated by
Tim Hildebrandt

Retold by **JIM LAWRENCE** and **TIM HILDEBRANDT**

DERRYDALE BOOKS
NewYork • Avenel, New Jersey

Santa's workshop at the North Pole was as busy as a beehive. Santa's helpers were sewing, hammering, and painting toys every color of the rainbow!

Then Mrs. Claus noticed that some of the toymakers were not at their workbenches. "Where are the Black Forest elves?" she asked.

"They were homesick, poor fellows," said Santa Claus. "They probably went back to their village for a visit."

"But Christmas is coming," his wife said irritably, "and there's so much to be done!"

"Oh, I'm sure they'll manage to do the work I've assigned them!" the jolly old fellow replied with a twinkle in his eye.

In another workshop, far from the North Pole, sat Heinrich, the shoemaker. He had used all but his last scrap of leather and he had no money to buy more.

"Oh dear! Whatever will we do when that last piece of leather is gone?" asked his good wife anxiously.

"There, there! Do not worry, my dear," said Heinrich. "We will manage somehow." And he cut the leather for one last pair of shoes.

When the shoemaker and his wife went into the workshop the next morning, they had a wonderful surprise! The last piece of leather had been sewn into a beautiful pair of shoes.

The shoes were so well made they fetched a high price. With the money he earned, Heinrich was able to buy enough leather for two more pairs of shoes.

That night, again, he cut the leather, but this time for two pairs of shoes. When he went to bed he left the pieces on his workbench.

The next morning, Mr. and Mrs. Heinrich could hardly believe their eyes. There were two more pairs of shoes on the workbench. They were so beautifully made they looked like the work of a master craftsman.

These shoes, too, were snapped up by eager buyers. So
Heinrich was able to buy still more leather. And, just as
before, the pieces he cut out were fashioned overnight into

shoes of beautiful workmanship. Soon, people
from all over the countryside were coming to
Heinrich's shop to buy his beautiful shoes.

"I wonder who is helping us," said Mrs. Heinrich one evening.

The shoemaker shrugged. "I can't imagine, my dear. It's a mystery to me, too."

"Then we must find out," said his wife. "Let us wait up tonight and see!"

"A good idea," said Heinrich with a smile. "We will stay out of sight and keep very quiet so we don't scare away our good friend, whoever he might be."

What a surprise the shoemaker
and his wife had when they peeked out
from their bedroom that night! There were five little elves
busily making shoes.

Mr. and Mrs. Heinrich tiptoed back to bed before the
elves could see them.

"What kind hearts those little fellows have!" said Heinrich the next morning. "How can we ever repay them?"

"I know!" said his wife. "I'll make

each of them a fine new suit of clothes—and knit stockings to match!"

"A wonderful idea," said Heinrich. "And I shall make them each a beautiful pair of little shoes!"

By Christmas Eve the presents for the elves were all ready. Heinrich hung the little shoes on the mantelpiece. His wife hung the little clothes and the little stockings on the Christmas tree.

That night it was the elves' turn to be surprised. Never before had anyone made *them* Christmas presents!

The shoemaker and his wife watched from their hiding place as their little friends tried on their new suits and stockings and shoes. Everything fit perfectly. When the elves were all dressed in their new clothes they danced merrily around the Christmas tree.

Now the work of the elves was done. The shoemaker
and his wife watched from the window as the little folks
danced out into the street.

Mrs. Heinrich sighed and squeezed her husband's
hand. "How wonderful that those good little people came
to help us," she murmured, "just when we needed help so
badly. I wonder who sent them."